The Sorcerer's
Apprentice

and other stories

First published in 2002 by Miles Kelly Publishing,
Bardfield Centre, Great Bardfield, Essex CM7 4SL

24681097531

Copyright © Miles Kelly Publishing Ltd 2002

Project manager: Paula Borton
Editorial Assistant: Nicola Sail

British Library Cataloguing-in-Publication Data
A catalogue record for this book is available from the British Library

ISBN 1-84236-092-2

Printed in Hong Kong

Visit us on the web:
www.mileskelly.net
Info@mileskelly.net

The Sorcerer's Apprentice
and other stories

Chosen by Fiona Waters

Miles Kelly
PUBLISHING

Contents

The Lion and the Mouse

a retelling from Aesop's Fables

The lion was very hungry. As he padded through the tall grass, something rustled by his feet. He reached out a great paw, and there was a squeak. He had caught a tiny mouse by the tail.

"Oh please let me go, dear lion," cried the tiny mouse. "I should be no more than a single mouthful for you. And I promise I will be able to help you some day."

The lion roared with laughter. The thought of a tiny mouse being able to help such a huge creature as himself amused him so much that he did let the mouse go.

"He would not have made much of a meal anyway," smiled the lion.

The mouse scuttled away, calling out to the lion,

"I shall not forget my promise!"

Many days and nights later the lion was padding through the tall grass again when he suddenly fell into a deep pit. A net was flung over him, and he lay there helpless, caught by some hunters. He twisted and turned but he could not free himself. The hunters just laughed at his struggles and went off to fetch a cart to carry the great lion back to their village.

As he lay there, the lion heard a tiny voice in his ear.

"I promised you I would be able to help you one day."

It was the tiny mouse! And straight away he began to gnaw through the rope that held the lion fast. He gnawed and chewed, and chewed and gnawed, and eventually he chewed and gnawed right through the rope and the lion was free. With a great bound, he leapt out of the pit and then reached back, very gently, to lift the tiny mouse out too.

"I shall never forget you, mouse. Thank you for remembering your promise and saving me," purred the great lion.

So the tiny mouse was able to help the great lion. One good turn deserves another, you see?

The Star Maiden and the Flax Flowers

an Austrian fairytale

Peter the goatherd lived high up a mountainside with his mother in a little wooden house. A fast flowing river dashed down the valley, lush green meadows on either side. These meadows were full of flowers, bluebells, daisies and buttercups. In the summer, Peter took the goats even higher up into the mountains to the small patches of green grass that grew among the rocks. The goats wore bells round their necks, and all day long these bells would jingle as the goats leapt from rock to rock. In the evening, Peter would play his pipes and the goats would all gather round him for the journey back to the house and the barn where Peter's mother would milk them.

One evening as they all trotted back down into the

barn, Peter's mother called out to him.

"Where is the white nanny goat and her two kids?"

Peter looked round. They were not there.

"I saw them as we came down the valley, I will go and look for them," he said as he turned and blew his pipes again, calling over the meadow. But they did not appear. Peter set off up the mountain track again. He knew he had to find the goats before it grew too dark: climbing over the rocks would be a dangerous task with only the stars to guide his steps. He did not dare leave looking until the morning as he was afraid a wolf might snatch them away.

He climbed higher and higher, playing his pipes all the while, but he could not find a trace of the nanny goat and her kids. All night he searched without any luck. But in the summer the nights are not long, and just as he thought he could go no further, the rising sun tipped the mountain tops with pink. He sat down exhausted and closed his eyes for a moment. He heard the first calls of the birds as the light gradually crept over the grey rocks. And as he listened, he heard a soft voice calling his name.

"Peter, Peter," and with the

voice he heard a gentle bleating. He leapt to his feet and looked all round. He could see no sign of the goats. The voice came again.

"Peter, Peter," and as he looked up at the rocks above him, he saw a beautiful girl, dressed in a long blue cloak. Her eyes were blue too, as blue as the morning sky. She stood in front of a cave Peter could not remember seeing before. From underneath her cloak peeped the white nanny goat and her two kids.

"Call them, Peter," she said and he put the pipe to his lips and blew a joyous tune. The nanny goat and her two kids bounded down to stand by his side. Peter stroked their rough heads and looked up to the girl. She was so beautiful, he felt quite tongue-tied. She smiled at him and laughed gently.

"You are a good goatherd, Peter. I have watched over you and your herd for many a long day. When I found your nanny and her two kids last evening I brought them up here to keep them safe from the wild beasts through the night."

Peter was still silent. He was so overcome he couldn't even find the words to say thank you to the beautiful girl with the blue eyes. She beckoned him towards the cave.

"I should like to give you a gift to remember me by, Peter. Would you like to choose, look inside the cave," she said as she stood aside. Peter gasped. Inside the cave there were great mounds of precious stones, diamonds, rubies and emeralds. Peter finally found his tongue.

"Who are you?" he whispered.

"I am Hertha, the Star Maiden," the girl replied. "I look

after all the little ones, the kids, the lambs, the little rabbits and the birds in the air, the new leaves and flowers, even the babies in the cradles. Now Peter, all these precious stones come from deep inside the earth, so what will you have?"

"My mother and I have all we need. We have food and clothes and our little wooden house. We have our goats and their kids. We have no need of precious stones," Peter said proudly.

The girl seemed very pleased with this reply.

"Good, Peter! I am pleased to see you are content but I would still like to give you something."

Peter smiled shyly at her.

"I should like some of those beautiful blue flowers growing by the entrance to the cave."

Peter had never seen the flowers before, they had slender stems and sky blue flowers, just the colour of the girl's eyes. She clapped her hands in delight.

"That is my very own flower, Peter. It is called flax. I shall give you some seeds to sow as well and my flowers will bring much good to you and your people." And she gave Peter a handful of tiny golden seeds. As he looked at them lying in his hand, the girl's cloak billowed around her and she was gone. So was the cave with all the precious stones, but there at his feet was a bunch of the pale blue flowers. Peter and the goats went happily downhill back to the little wooden house where his mother was waiting anxiously for him.

Peter planted the golden seeds, and the next year the flax bloomed like a blue cloud in the valley. Then early one mid-summer morning, Hertha suddenly appeared and showed them how to dry and then comb the flax to make it into linen. And so the little blue flowers were indeed a gift that brought much good to everyone.

The Magic Porridge Pot

a Swedish folk tale

This is the story of an old porridge pot. One day, just before Christmas, a poor old farmer and his wife decided that they needed to sell their last cow as they had no money left, and no food in the cupboard. As the farmer walked sadly to market with the cow, he met a very strange little man on the road. He had a long white beard right down to his toes, which were bare, and he wore a huge black hat, under which the farmer could only just see the bright gleam of his eyes. Over his arm he carried a battered old porridge pot.

"That's a nice looking cow," said the strange little man. "Is she for sale?"

"Yes," said the farmer.

"I shall buy your cow," declared the strange little man, putting the porridge pot down with a thump. "I shall give you this porridge pot in exchange for your cow!"

Well, the farmer looked at the battered old porridge pot, and he looked at his fine cow. And he was just about to say, "Certainly not!" when a voice whispered, "Take me! Take me!"

The farmer shook himself. Dear me, it was bad enough to be poor without beginning to hear strange voices. He opened his mouth again to say, "Certainly not!" when he heard the voice again. "Take me! Take me!"

Well, he saw at once that it must be a magic pot, and he knew you didn't hang about with magic pots, so he said very quickly to the strange little man, "Certainly!" and handed over the cow. He bent down to pick up the pot, and when he looked up, the strange little man had vanished into thin air.

The farmer knew he was going to have a difficult time explaining to his wife just how he had come to part with their precious cow for a battered old porridge pot.

She was very angry indeed and had started to say a lot of very cross things when a voice came from the pot,

"Take me inside and clean me and polish me, and you shall see what you shall see!"

Well, the farmer's wife was astonished but she did as she was bid. She washed the pot inside and out, and then she polished it until it shone as bright as a new pin. No sooner had she finished than the pot hopped off the table, and straight out of the door. The farmer and his wife sat down by the fire, not saying a word to each other. They had no money, no cow, no food and now it seemed they didn't even have their magic pot.

Down the road from the poor farmer, there lived a rich man. He was a selfish man who spent all his time eating huge meals and counting his money. He had lots of servants, including a cook who was in the kitchen making a Christmas pudding. The pudding was stuffed with plums, currants, sultanas, almonds and goodness knows what else. It

was so big that the cook realised she didn't have a pot to boil it in. It was at this point that the porridge pot trotted in the door.

"Goodness me!" she exclaimed. "The fairies must have sent this pot just in time to take my pudding," and she dropped the pudding in the pot. No sooner had the pudding fallen to the bottom with a very satisfying thud, than the pot skipped out of the door again. The cook gave a great shriek, but by the time the butler and the footman and the parlour maid and the boy who turned the spit had all dashed into the kitchen, the pot was quite out of sight.

The porridge pot in the meantime trotted down the road to the poor farmer's house. He and his wife were delighted to see the pot again, and even more pleased when they discovered the wonderful pudding. The wife boiled it up and it lasted them for three days. So they had a good Christmas after all, while the old porridge pot sat quietly by the fire.

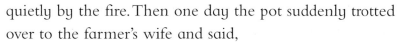

Spring came, and still the porridge pot sat quietly by the fire. Then one day the pot suddenly trotted over to the farmer's wife and said,

"Clean me, and polish me, and you shall see what you shall see."

So the farmer's wife polished the pot till it shone as bright as a new pin.

No sooner had she finished than the pot hopped off the table, and straight out of the door.

You will remember that the rich man was very fond of counting his money. There he sat in the great hall, with piles of golden guineas and silver sixpences on the table, and great bulging bags of coins on the floor at his feet. He was wondering where he could hide the money when in trotted the pot. Now the cook had been far too frightened of the rich man's temper to tell him about the pot stealing the Christmas pudding, so when he saw the pot he was delighted.

"Goodness me!" he exclaimed, "The fairies must have sent this pot just in time to take my money," and he dropped several bags of money in the pot. No sooner had

the bags fallen to the bottom with a very satisfying clink, than the pot skipped out of the door again. The rich man shouted and hollered, but by the time the coachman and the head groom and the stable lad had run into the great hall, the pot was quite out of sight.

It trotted down the road to the poor farmer's house. He and his wife were delighted to see the pot again, and even more pleased when they discovered the bags of gold and silver. There was enough money to last them for the rest of their days, even after they had bought a new cow.

As for the battered old porridge pot, it sat quietly by the fire for many a long year. Then, one day, it suddenly trotted straight out of the door. It went off up the road until it was out of sight, and the farmer and his wife never saw it again.

The Greedy Dog

an English tale

There was once a very greedy dog who just ate and ate. Whenever he saw anything that looked good enough to eat, he would just open his mouth and gobble it all up. The postman wouldn't come near the house anymore, ever since the greedy dog mistook his ankle for an early breakfast. He would stand at the gate and throw the letters in the general direction of the letterbox. The paperboy just refused to go anywhere near. Visitors knew they had to come with a juicy bone or they wouldn't get as far as the front door.

One day the greedy dog was out wandering round the shops. He loved doing this as there were always lots of really good smells for him to investigate, and sometimes old ladies, who didn't know any better, would give him sticky buns to eat.

As he walked past the butcher's shop, the greedy dog started to lick his lips. There in the window was a great big steak. It looked juicy and very good to eat. The greedy dog decided that the steak would make a very nice meal. So he watched and waited outside the shop. Soon one of his favourite old ladies walked down the street and into the butcher's shop. The greedy dog sidled in alongside the unsuspecting old lady. She wanted sausages and mince and goodness knows what else, so while the butcher was looking after her, the greedy dog pounced. He grabbed the steak and galloped out of the shop before anyone really had time to realise what was happening.

Then there was a great hue and cry. The butcher ran out of his shop with a bellow of rage, the little old lady fainted, and everyone in the street joined in the chase. But the greedy dog knew all the back streets, and he was soon far away and longing to eat his steak. He ran through the back streets until he came to the canal. He was just about to cross the bridge when he caught sight of another dog, right in front of him, and this dog also had a great juicy steak in his mouth! Well now, you and I know that what he was looking at was his own reflection, but the greedy dog did not know that. All he saw was a second steak that he might have so, with a great fierce bark, he leapt at the other dog.

But instead of gaining another meal, the greedy dog found himself very wet indeed, and he had lost his own steak! It would be good if I could tell you that from that day onwards the greedy dog was better behaved. But I am afraid his manners did not improve, and he is still looking for the other dog. . .

Goldilocks and the Three Bears

a retelling from the original tale by Andrew Lang

Once upon a time there was a little girl called Goldilocks who lived in the middle of a great forest with her mother and her father. Now ever since she was tiny, her mother had told her she must never, ever wander off into the forest for it was full of wild creatures, especially bears. But as Goldilocks grew older she longed to explore the forest.

One washday, when her mother was busy in the kitchen, hidden in clouds of steam, Goldilocks sneaked off down the path that led deep into the forest.

At first she was happy, looking at the wild flowers and listening to the birds singing, but it did not take long for her to become hopelessly lost.

She wandered for hours and hours and, as it grew darker, she became frightened. She started to cry, but then she saw a light shining through the trees. She rushed forward, sure she had somehow found her way home, only to realise that it was not her own cottage that she was looking at. But she opened the door and looked inside.

On a scrubbed wooden table there were three bowls of steaming hot porridge; a big one, a middle-sized one and a little one. Goldilocks was so tired that she quite forgot all her manners and just sat down at the table. The big bowl was too tall for her to reach. The middle-sized bowl was too hot. But the little one was just right, so she ate all the porridge up.

By the warm fire there were three chairs: a big one, a middle-sized one and a little one. Goldilocks couldn't climb up into the big one. The middle-sized one was too hard. The

little was just the right size, but as soon as she sat down, it broke into pieces. Goldilocks scrambled to her feet and then noticed there were steps going upstairs, where she found three beds: a big one, a middle-sized one and a little one. The big bed was too hard. The middle-sized one was too soft. But the little one was just right and she was soon fast asleep.

The cottage belonged to three bears, and it was not long before they came home. They knew at once that someone had been inside.

Father Bear growled,

"Who has been eating my porridge?"

Mother Bear grumbled,

"Who has been eating my porridge?"

And Baby Bear gasped,

"Who has been eating my porridge, AND has eaten it all up?"

The bears looked round the room. They looked at the chairs by the warm fire.

Father Bear growled,

"Who has been sitting in my chair?"

Mother Bear grumbled,

"Who has been sitting in my chair?"

And Baby Bear gasped,

"Who has been sitting in my chair, AND has broken it to bits?"

The bears all clumped upstairs. They looked at the three beds.

Father Bear growled,

"Who has been sleeping in my bed?"

Mother Bear grumbled,

"Who has been sleeping in my bed?"

And Baby Bear gasped,

"Who has been sleeping in my bed, AND is still there?"

Suddenly Goldilocks woke up. All she could see was three very cross-looking bears. She jumped off the bed, ran down the stairs, and out of the door. She ran and ran and ran, and by good fortune found herself outside her own cottage. Her mother and father scolded, but then gave her lots of hugs and kisses, and a big bowl of soup. Goldilocks had certainly learnt her lesson, and she never ever wandered off again.

The Cat and the Mouse

a retelling from the original story by the Brothers Grimm

Now this is the tale of a wily cat and a foolish mouse. The mouse lived in a bare mouse hole under the pulpit in the church. The cat lived on an old cushion in the vestry. They had met on several occasions, the mouse usually whisking herself away very fast to the safety of her hole. She did not like the look of the cat's claws.

But one day, the cat called on the mouse at home.

"Miss mouse," a purry voice said, "why don't you and I set up home together? We could live in the bell tower and look after each other. We could share our food, too."

The mouse thought

about this carefully. She had never been fond of cats ever since her great grandfather had been supper for the farm tom cat one cold frosty night. But she could see that there would be benefits. The cat had a nice smile on his face. So she agreed.

They put their savings together and bought a pot full of fat for the winter. The cat said he would hide it away safely under the altar where no one ever went, and so it was done. They both promised not to touch it until the weather became really bad.

The mouse went about her business, quite happy in her new home, although she found the stairs a wearisome business. But the cat could not stop thinking about the pot of fat. So he thought up a plan.

"Miss mouse, my cousin has just had a kitten," he said looking at the mouse with his green eyes. "And she would like me to be godcat. I should like to go to the christening, would you mind?"

"Not at all, Mister cat," said the mouse. "I have plenty to do today."

But the wicked Cat went straight to the pot of fat and ate the top off. Then he went to sleep for the rest of the day. When it was evening, he stretched and strolled back up to the bell tower.

"Did you have a nice time?" asked the mouse

"Oh yes, very nice," said the not very nice cat.

"And what is the kitten called?"

"Topoff," replied the cat.

"Topoff?" asked the mouse. "That is a very strange name. Still I suppose cats have different family names," and she went on with her work.

All went quietly for a few days but then the cat had great longings for the pot of fat again so he went to the mouse.

"I find I have another new godkitten. Would you mind if I went to the christening?" said the cat, his green eyes half closed.

"Another godkitten?" said the mouse. "My, my you do have a big family."

And the beastly cat slunk off and ate up half the pot of fat. When he sauntered back up the stairs that night the mouse was waiting.

"Well, how did it all go?" she said. "What is this kitten to be called?"

"Halfempty," replied the cat.

"Halfempty?" said the mouse. "I have never heard such a thing before."

But the cat was asleep, a secret smile twitching his whiskers.

Well, as you can imagine, it was not long before that greedy cat wanted some fat again.

"Miss mouse, just imagine! I have yet another godkitten. I should really go to this christening too," said the cat.

Miss mouse thought it all very strange but she was a kindly creature so she waved the cat off to yet another christening. The cat, of course, just scuttled downstairs, slid under the altar and licked the pot of fat quite clean. He came back very late that night.

"Now what strange name did your family give this new kitten?" asked the mouse crossly. She had a headache from all the noise in the tower when the bells rang.

"Allgone," said the cat.

"Topoff, Halfempty and now Allgone!" the Mouse said

in disbelief. "Well, I am very glad I am not a member of your family. I couldn't be doing with such weird names," and she went to sleep with her paws over her ears.

There were no more christenings for a while. The weather became colder and colder, and the mouse began to think of the little pot of fat hidden under the altar.

"Mister cat," she said one frosty morning, "I think it is time we collected our pot of fat. I am looking forward to a lick."

We will see about that thought the cat, but he padded downstairs behind the mouse. She reached under the altar and brought out the pot, but of course when she looked in it was all empty.

"What a foolish mouse I have been!" she cried. "Now I see what a wicked cat you have been. Topoff, Halfempty and Allgone indeed!"

"Such is the way of cats," said the greedy cat, and he put out a paw to grab mouse. But she was too quick for him, and dived back into her dear little mouse hole under the pulpit.

Never again did she trust cats, ever, ever.

The Moon Caught in the Marsh

a folk tale from East Anglia

The Moon looked down on the marsh. It was oozy and murky, and people were afraid to cross the marsh at night unless the Moon was shining. It was said that on dark nights the marsh goblins would lead travellers astray and drag them down into the clinging black mud.

Now the Moon did not believe these tales but she decided to see for herself. She wrapped herself in a great dark cloak and slipped down to the marsh. All you could see was her tiny silver feet below the cloak.

But the goblins could see in the dark. As soon as they saw the Moon's silver feet they all crept up close to her and tried to pull at the great cloak with their horrid cold hands. The Moon realised exactly what the travellers had to put up with. And then she heard a cry coming from quite close by. It was a poor man who had come to fetch the doctor for his wife who was going to have a baby. In the deep dark he had tripped over a tree root and hurt his foot.

The beastly goblins ran away from the Moon the moment they heard the man cry out and they began pushing and pulling him here, there and everywhere. The man yelled out in fear, and the Moon was so upset that she flung aside her cloak and shone out in all her bright glory. The goblins scattered, their eyes hurting from the brilliance of the Moon.

The man escaped from the marsh and ran all the way to the doctor, in the clear moonlight. And later that night, his wife safely produced a beautiful little girl with shining white hair. Everyone always said she looked like a moonbeam.

But the Moon was still in the marsh, and she found her tiny silver feet were stuck in the mud. She turned this way and that, but she could not get out. And then she stumbled and fell with a splash into the dark black mud. Instantly her glorious light went out. With wicked cries of delight the

goblins all came
running back, and
rolled a great flat
stone over the
spot where the
Moon lay
trapped. Not
a single
beam of her
light was to
be seen.

Days went
by, and then weeks.
The villagers waited anxiously
for the new Moon but there was no sign of it. When a
month had gone by, several of the villagers gathered
together to decide what to do. The man who had been
rescued the night his daughter was born suggested that
perhaps the Moon might be found near where he had been
caught by the goblins. They set off towards the spot, bravely
determined to find out what had happened to the Moon.
They all carried flaring torches and sang bold songs to
cheer themselves.

When they reached the spot the first thing they saw
was the great flat stone. The next thing they saw was
hundreds and hundreds of nasty spiteful goblins. The goblins
tried to blow out the torches, but the men re-lit them as fast

as ever possible. The men waded out into the marsh and with a huge effort lifted the side of the great stone. Out shone a blinding ray of moonlight. The goblins all disappeared, shrieking in dismay. Slowly, slowly the men lifted the stone and the grateful Moon sailed high into the sky once more. She shone down on the men as they walked home, and she shone the next night, and the next. Best of all, from that day forth there was never a goblin to be seen or heard in that part of the country.

The Sorcerer's Apprentice

a German folk tale

The sorcerer lived in a dusty room at the top of a very tall gloomy tower. His table was covered with bottles and jars full of strange-coloured potions, and bubbling mixtures filled the air with horrible smells. The walls of the tower were lined with huge old books. These were the sorcerer's spell books and he would let no one else look inside them.

The sorcerer had a young apprentice called Harry. He was a good but lazy boy who longed only to be able to do magic himself. The sorcerer had promised to teach him all he knew, but only when he thought Harry was ready.

One day the sorcerer had to visit a friend who was a warlock. The sorcerer had never left Harry alone in the tower before and he did not entirely trust him. Looking very fierce, the sorcerer gave Harry his instructions.

"I have a very important spell to conjure up tonight when I return, so I need the cauldron full of water from the well," he said. "When you have filled the cauldron, you can sweep the floor and then you must light the fire."

Harry was not best pleased. It would take many, many trips to the well to fill the cauldron, and he would have all those steps to climb each time. Perhaps the sorcerer could read his mind, for the last thing he said as he climbed out of the window to fly away on his small green dragon was, "Touch nothing!" and off he flew in a cloud of smoke and flame from the dragon.

Harry watched until the sorcerer was safely far out of sight, and then did precisely what

he had been told not to
do. He took down one
of the old dusty spell
books. For a while
all was quiet in the
tower, and then
Harry found what
he was looking for.
It was a spell to
make a broomstick
obey orders. Harry didn't
hesitate. He forgot the sorcerer's
instructions, he forgot that magic can
be very dangerous. He took the broomstick
in one hand and the spell book in the other,
and read out the spell in a quavery voice for,
truth to tell, he was very nervous. Nothing
happened. Harry tried again, and this time his voice
was stronger.

The broomstick quivered and then stood up. It
grabbed a bucket and jumped off down the stairs. Soon it
was back, the bucket brimful of water which it tipped into
the cauldron. Harry was delighted and smiled as the
broomstick set off down the stairs again. Up and down the
broomstick went and soon the cauldron was full.

"Stop, stop!" shouted Harry, but the broomstick just
carried on, and on. Soon the floor was awash and then the

bottles and jars were floating around the room. Nothing Harry could say would stop the broomstick, and so in desperation, he grabbed the axe that lay by the fireside and chopped the broomstick into pieces. To his horror, all the pieces of wood turned into new broomsticks and they set off downstairs to the well, buckets appearing magically in their hands.

By now the water was nearly up to the ceiling. Wet spell books spun round and round the room, and Harry gave himself up for lost. Suddenly there was a great clatter of wings and a hiss of steam as the green dragon flew into the tower. The sorcerer was back! In a huge voice he commanded the broomsticks to stop. They did. Then he ordered the water back into the well. It all rushed back down the stairs. Then he ordered the dragon to dry everything with its hot breath. Then he turned to look at Harry. And, oh dear! Harry could see that the sorcerer was very, very angry indeed. The sorcerer looked as if he might turn Harry into something terrible, but then he sat down on a soggy cushion with a squelch.

"Right, I think it is time I taught you how to do magic PROPERLY!" And he did.

Peter and the Wolf

original libretto by Sergey Prokofiev

Peter lived with his grandfather at the edge of the forest. Peter used to play with the wild birds and animals in the garden, but his grandfather always warned him not to go into the meadow in case the wolf crept out of the forest.

I am afraid Peter did not always do as he was told, so one day he slipped through the garden gate and into the meadow when he met a duck swimming in the middle of the pond.

"You must watch out for the wolf," said Peter to the duck but she was too busy enjoying herself to listen. Round and round the pond she swam. A little bird flew

down and the duck tried to persuade her to come into the pond as well. But as the little bird stood talking to the duck, Peter saw the cat sneak up behind her.

"Look out!" shouted Peter and the bird flew up to safety in the tree.

"Thank you, Peter," she said. The cat was not so pleased. Just then Peter's grandfather came out and saw the open garden gate.

"Peter! How many times do I have to tell you? Come back into the garden at once," he shouted and Peter walked slowly back in.

Meanwhile, at the far side of the meadow, nearest the forest, a grey shape slunk out from under the trees. It was the wolf!

The little bird flew up into the tree, and the cat joined her, although on a lower branch. But the duck was too busy swimming to see what was happening and in a flash the wolf grabbed her and swallowed her whole!

Peter saw it all from the garden.

"I am going to catch that old wolf," he said to himself.

He found a piece of rope and climbed up a tree whose branches overhung the meadow. He made a loop in the rope and hung it out of the tree. Then he called to the little bird, "Can you tempt the

wolf this way by flying round his head, please? I am going to catch him!"

The brave little bird darted down very close to the wolf's nose. The wolf snapped his fierce teeth, and only just missed the little bird. Closer and closer they came to the tree where Peter was hiding. The wolf was so busy trying to catch the bird that he did not see the rope. Peter looped it over the wolf's tail, and there he was, dangling from the branch of the tree!

Peter's grandfather came out and he was astonished to see the wolf. Just then some hunters came out of the forest.

"Well done," they cried, "you have caught the wolf. We have been after him for a long time."

And they all went off in a very joyful procession to the zoo. Peter led the wolf at the front, the little bird flew overhead, and the cat padded alongside, taking care not to get too close to the wolf. The hunters came up in the rear with Peter's grandfather. And from deep inside the wolf's tummy, the duck quacked loudly, just to remind everyone that she was there!

How Jumbo went to the Moon

an English tale first told by Joyce M Westrup 1936

Jumbo was a dog, a small woolly dog with a great plume of a tail. He belonged to two brothers who had decided after travelling the world that they wanted to settle down. So they looked for a place to build a house. They searched and searched and searched, and eventually they found just the right spot. They had discovered a little clearing in a great green forest, with a stream running by.

"This is the spot!" said the brothers to Jumbo and they all began work straight away on their new house. Jumbo didn't do very much other than run around barking, but he thought he was helping. The brothers cleared a big square in the grass, and then the eldest brother took his great axe and began chopping down a tall tree for the roof.

A huge great voice said, "Who said you could chop

down my trees?" and a
big ugly face looked
down at the brothers
and Jumbo from
above the tree. It was
a giant, and he looked
very cross.

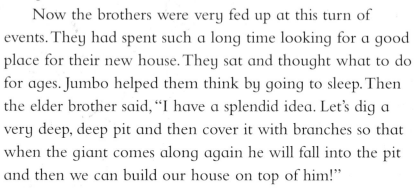

"We wanted to
build our new house
here," said the younger
brother bravely.

"Well, you can't!"
said the giant and he
stumped off back into the forest.

Now the brothers were very fed up at this turn of
events. They had spent such a long time looking for a good
place for their new house. They sat and thought what to do
for ages. Jumbo helped them think by going to sleep. Then
the elder brother said, "I have a splendid idea. Let's dig a
very deep, deep pit and then cover it with branches so that
when the giant comes along again he will fall into the pit
and then we can build our house on top of him!"

So they set to, and Jumbo helped with the digging
because he was good at that. Soon their giant trap was
ready, and the elder brother took up his great axe again.
He had only chopped his third chop when the giant came
stomping down the path shouting at the top of his huge

voice, "I thought I told you not to… HELP!" he yelled as
he fell down the deep, deep pit. Well, it was a very deep,
deep pit and the giant just could not get out. The two
brothers cut down lots more trees and soon they had built a
very nice house indeed, right over the deep, deep pit. They
made a trap door in the kitchen floor so they could send
down meals to the giant. The brothers were quite kind-
hearted in this way, and it was the giant's forest after all.

Now the giant was quite well brought up, but the one
thing he was very bad about was
eating his crusts. He just dropped
these onto the floor of the pit,
and before long he was knee
deep in crusts.
Then he had a
splendid idea.

He piled all the
crusts up into one
great heap, and
when he climbed up
this heap he found
he could reach the
trap door. He
pushed the trap
door open very
carefully and
scrambled out.

He found it was night-time and everybody, including Jumbo, was fast asleep. The giant bent down and scooped up the entire house in his great arms and he hurled it up, high, high into the sky. The two brothers landed on a star each, but Jumbo fell on the moon. They are all quite happy up there, and if you look very carefully sometimes you can see Jumbo, waving his great plume of a tail. I don't know what happened to the giant but I am sure it was a long time before anyone dared try to build a house in his forest again!